Jellybean Books™

Theodore's Best Friend

by Mary Man-Kong

illustrated by Ken Edwards

W9-BIO-531

Based on the script by Kathy MacLellan

From the *Theodore Tugboat* series created by Andrew Cochran

Random House 🏠 New York

Library of Congress Catalog Card Number: 98-66212. First Random House Jellybean Books™ edition, 1999.
ISBN: 0-679-89409-8 (trade); 0-679-99409-2 (lib.bdg.)   www.randomhouse.com/kids
JELLYBEAN BOOKS is a trademark of Random House, Inc.

Printed in the United States of America   10 9 8 7 6 5 4 3 2 1

One day, Emily was telling Theodore all about her trip across the ocean. She'd seen many interesting things. Theodore was impressed.

"Emily, you're my best friend," he said.

"Thank you," said Emily, and off she went with a very happy smile.

"Race you around Bedford Buoy!" Hank called out to Theodore. The two tugs were off before you could say, "One—toot!"

Hank made the fastest turns Theodore had ever seen. Theodore was amazed.

"Hank, you're my best friend!" he said.

"Great!" said Hank, racing ahead. "I've always wanted to have a best friend."

Ping! Ping! went Foduck's sonar machine. "There's a sandbar here," Foduck said. "The water isn't very deep. A tugboat could get stuck! I've got to warn the others."

Just then Theodore saw Foduck's new red lifeboat.

"What a great lifeboat!" Theodore said.

"We could trade," said Foduck. "I'll lend you my lifeboat and you lend me yours."

Theodore felt so happy that he blurted out, "Foduck, you're my best friend!"

Just then Hank churned by.

"Where did you get that red lifeboat, Theodore?" asked Hank.

"We traded lifeboats," Foduck said. "Theodore's my best friend."

"But Theodore's *my* best friend," said Hank.

Everyone was quiet, especially Theodore.

"Oh, well," said Hank sadly, floating away. "I have to go practice my speed turns."

Theodore knew Hank was upset, but he didn't know what to do.

That afternoon, the Dispatcher announced that three big ships would be arriving. All the tugboats were needed.

But where was Hank?

The four tugboats went off to find him.

Theodore found Hank first.

"Hank!" Theodore called. "We have a big job this afternoon!"

But Hank didn't move. He didn't even answer.

Theodore went to get help. He told Emily about Hank.

"Why won't he talk to you?" asked Emily.

"I told Hank he was my best friend," Theodore said, "but then I said Foduck was my best friend."

Emily frowned. "But I thought *I* was your best friend!"

"We've found Hank," called George. "He's stuck on a sandbar."

The other tugboats went to help—but Theodore stayed behind.

"It's all because of me," Theodore said. "All these problems are because of me."

"C'mon, Theodore," George puffed. "We need your help!"
Theodore sped over to join the others.
"One! Two! *Three!*" George roared.
Hank was finally free!
"Hooray!" everyone whistled. Theodore's whistle was the loudest.

"How did you get stuck?" Emily asked.

"I was practicing speed turns," Hank explained. "But I was thinking about Theodore not being my best friend and I plowed right into the sandbar."

"Is that why you didn't answer me when I called you?" asked Theodore. "I didn't even hear you," Hank said. "I was facing the other way!"

HANK

THEODORE

"So who *is* your best friend, Theodore?" Emily asked.
Theodore didn't know what to say. Emily knew so
many things. Hank was lots of fun. Foduck was always
solving problems. George had such a big heart…

Then Theodore remembered how good it felt when all the tugs helped rescue Hank.

"I know," tooted Theodore. "We're *all* best friends!"